FOLLOW ME!

NANCY TAFURI

GREENWILLOW BOOKS · NEW YORK

FOR CRISTINA

Watercolor inks and a black pen were used for the full-color art.

Copyright © 1990 by Nancy Tafuri. All rights reserved.
No part of this book may be reproduced or utilized in any form or
by any means, electronic or mechanical, including photocopying,
recording, or by any information storage and retrieval system,
without permission in writing from the Publisher, Greenwillow Books,
a division of William Morrow & Company, Inc., 105 Madison Avenue,
New York, NY 10016.   First Edition
10 9 8 7 6 5 4 3 2 1

Printed in Hong Kong by South China Printing Company (1988) Ltd.

Library of Congress Cataloging-in-Publication Data
Tafuri, Nancy.   Follow me!
Summary: A sea lion follows a wandering crab to an entire colony
of crabs and then returns to its fellow sea lions.
[1. Sea lions—Fiction.   2. Crabs—Fiction]   I. Title.
PZ7.T117Fo   1990   [E]   89-23259
ISBN 0-688-08773-6   ISBN 0-688-08774-4 (lib. bdg.)